Just Wilberfor

Written and illustrated by Racey Helps

PINNY NEEDLEKIN PONSONBY WILBERFORCE DIGGY WINKS HOPPY SPARROW

©The Medici Society Ltd., London 1970. Printed in England Code 85503005 4

2

Whenever Hoppy Sparrow flew near the Old Brick House, he would stop to perch on a certain window ledge and wave his wings cheerily at the captive inside. This was a white mouse in a cage. Hoppy felt sorry for him and made sure to visit him often, 'just to cheer him up'.

The mouse was called Wilberforce and he needed 'cheering up', for his mistress, a little girl named Sally, would sometimes forget about him, so that he often felt hungry and lonely.

Snowflake, the white cat, would sometimes stare longingly at Wilberforce. She did not like him. She thought that Sally neglected her because of "that silly mouse".

One day Sally's mother noticed that Wilberforce had no food. "Sally is *so* careless," she said crossly as she filled his food dish, closed the cage door—and forgot to fasten it!

When she had left, Wilberforce pushed open the cage door—and was FREE! He hopped onto the table, ran boldly across it and dropped to the floor. Along one side of the room was a dresser. No-one would think of looking for him there! He scrambled up and popped himself into a mug.

At the same time Hoppy fluttered down and looked through the window.

"Why, he's gone!" he told himself. "I must keep a sharp look out in case he needs help."

Wilberforce soon peeped over the rim of the mug. Delightedly he saw that the door was ajar and, almost as soon as it takes to tell, he was through and away.'

For the first time in his life Wilberforce found himself pushing his way through tall grasses. It was tiring work and he was glad when he found a clear patch where flowers grew beneath ferns.

"I see you are admiring my garden," said a voice behind him, and, looking round, he saw a mole beaming at him. The mole bowed—not too elegantly because of his plumpish shape—and Wilberforce bowed too. "How d'you do?" he said.

"I do nicely, thank you," grinned the mole. "I'm always pleased to meet folk who like pretty things like flowers."

"Yes, I *do* like pretty things," said Wilberforce. "Not that I've actually *owned* anything pretty, of course. What are these things called?"

"They are called Herb Tuppence," beamed the mole. "But tell me, why haven't you ever owned a pretty thing yourself?"

So Wilberforce explained how he had been shut away in a cage. The mole was shocked. "I'm awfully glad you managed to get away," he said. "But where are you going now?"

The mouse shook his head. "I don't know anywhere *to* go!" he said.

The mole took off his spectacles, polished them on his sleeve, and perched them back on his pink nose. He glimmered at Wilberforce through them for a moment or two, then:—"My name is Diggy Winks and I should very much like to help you. Would you like me to—well, to show you around?"

"That *is* kind of you," said Wilberforce. "I should like that very much. My name is Wilberforce."

"That's a nice name," beamed Diggy, nodding his head. "You look a bit tired, you know, so catch hold of my arm and I'll take you home for a cup of tea and a bite to eat."

By the time they reached Diggy's home Wilberforce was ready to drop with tiredness.

"Here we are!" said the mole. The world had gone dark and Wilberforce peered this way and that to try to see the house. "Come along in." And the mole led the way through a dim doorway and down a dark passage. "I don't know why one old mole should need so many rooms, I'm sure," said Diggy. "You haven't a home now, have you? So you must come to live here with me." He led the way into a room and lighted a lamp. "There," he said proudly, "what do you think of it?" Wilberforce was so overcome he could only squeak—and when the mole presented him with a coat to wear he couldn't even do that!

"Can you play the piano?" asked Diggy. "No? Pity. You see, although I love music my fingers are too clumsy to play myself." Now, it was the very next morning that the real ADVENTURE began! Leaving the mouse to get on with some dusting, the mole had set off to do the shopping. Hoppy the sparrow, who had been sitting on a branch enjoying the morning sun, saw him trudging up the lane. "Hello!" called out Hoppy. The mole waved his stick cheerily. "Hello, Hoppy!" he cried.

"You look very pleased this morning," chirruped Hoppy. Diggy explained all about Wilberforce and Hoppy soon realised he was talking about the White Mouse he used to "cheer up" through the window.

"I know your Wilberforce," he cried. "I'm *so* glad he really did escape from that horrid cage. I'll call around to see him one day." He watched Diggy tramp off along the lane humming a moley tune to himself. Then the sparrow gave a chirp of alarm, for skipping across the fields was Sally!

7

"Diggy Winks, run and hide!" cried Hoppy; but Sally had already caught sight of the little figure of the mole plodding along with his shopping basket. Poor Diggy! Before he knew what was happening Sally bent down and grabbed him.

"Why, it's a mole!" she laughed. "And it's dressed in real clothes! I never knew moles wore real clothes!"

"Let me go!" cried Diggy, struggling with all his might.

"Yes, let him go, let him go!" shouted Hoppy, fluttering round her head in a fury. Sally took no notice.

"This mole will make a nice new pet for me," she said. And she placed Diggy inside her pocket.

Hoppy knew he could not help Diggy on his own. "I'll get help," he panted, and off he flew.

Now Wilberforce had finished dusting and was having a wash-day. Perhaps it was because he had never used a bottle of detergent before, for as he scrubbed and rubbed, the foam rose and grew and grew and rose until the kitchen became full of floating bubbles. Every now and again he rushed round the kitchen hitting out with a broom to make them burst; and whenever they tickled his nose he burst whole batches with a huge sneeze. Afterwards he stood on a wash-tub hanging out the clothes to dry. There was a little breeze, just enough to dry them by tea-time, he thought. How pleased his friend Diggy would be when he returned to see all the things dancing a welcome on the line.

He thought he could hear the mole coming, but glancing over his shoulder he saw it was somebody hurrying towards him in a bright red coat; somehow he thought he had seen that red coat before.

"Sally's caught Diggy!" gulped Hoppy. Wilberforce gave a squeak. "There's no time to lose," cried the sparrow. "We must round up all Diggy's friends and then decide what must be done!" And he hurried off to look for Ponsonby the vole and Pinny the hedgehog. Wilberforce left his washing and ran off too . . .

Hoppy found Ponsonby and Pinny just about to enter a sweet-shop.

"It's Diggy—" panted Hoppy, and he gasped out the dreadful news.

"We must think of a plan to rescue him," said Ponsonby.

"But how? cried Hoppy. He told them all about the White Mouse being a friend of the mole's. "Oh dear, supposing the White Mouse tries to rescue Diggy all by himself!"

"Then Sally will have two pets in that cage!" gasped Pinny.

"I've got an idea!" cried Ponsonby. "You and I, Pinny, will run to the Old Brick House to see what we can do. You, Hoppy, must find Mr. Heron and ask him to help us. Ask him to wait near the gateway of the house so that he can carry us away fast if we should come running out."

"I'll ask him," nodded Hoppy, "but I don't see how he can carry all of you."

"What we want is a friendly pelican," muttered Pinny.

"I've thought it all out," said Ponsonby. "After you've spoken to Mr. Heron, Hoppy, run along to

Tippetty Nippet, the Squirrel. He's got a hanky a little boy once dropped which he uses as a sheet. Ask to borrow it and race with it to Mr. Heron."

Hoppy did not wait to hear more, and off he flew to find Mr. Heron, while Ponsonby and Pinny hastened towards the Old Brick House. When they got there, hot and dusty, they were just in time to see Wilberforce running up the garden path to the open front door. Before they could stop him he had hopped over the doorstep and disappeared.

Ponsonby and Pinny looked at each other glumly. "Now there are two of them to rescue," said Ponsonby.

"Unless he rescues Diggy all by himself," suggested Pinny, not very hopefully.

"He may, so we'll wait a little bit and see," decided Ponsonby. So they waited—and waited, but no-one came out and no-one went in; and at last Ponsonby could wait no longer.

"I'll go in by myself," he whispered, "and if I'm not out in five minutes, then you come in too."

Pinny watched round-eyed as his friend skipped up the path and into the house. Then he picked a dandelion clock.

"I'll blow once for every minute," he said to himself, "then I shall know when five minutes have gone by." He filled his cheeks, closed his eyes and blew. When he opened them again all he had left was the stalk. "Well, *that* was a quick five minutes," he muttered, and, throwing the stalk away, he tramped up the path and walked boldly in at the door.

"Ponsonby," he whispered, as quietly as he could, "where are you?" There was no reply.

Pinny crept along the hall and peered round the first open door he found. And there, on the carpet, lay a large white cat, gazing at him with unwinking eyes. Pinny's eyes did blink as he saw that the cat held the struggling forms of both the White Mouse and Ponsonby. Pinny thought hard—which was something he didn't do very often—and then he came into the room with a wide grin on his face.

"Good day, Mrs. Cat," he smirked. "I trust you are keeping well?"

"Ugh! a prickly hedgehog," said Snowflake. "And what do *you* want?"

Pinny made as low a bow as his fat tummy would allow. Ponsonby shouted at Pinny to run away and save himself.

"So you are a friend of these very silly mice," snapped Snowflake.

Pinny managed the bow again. "And your friend too, I'm sure," he giggled.

"*My* friend!" Snowflake shewed her teeth in a way that made Pinny a little uncomfortable. "Please go away," she said, "for I'm not going to share my supper with *anyone*."

"Oh, thank you for inviting me to dinner," said Pinny, "but really I could not manage it today. I've really come to see if my *three* friends are ready to come for a walk with me."

"Well, they *can't*!" snapped Snowflake. "And what do you mean, you horrid prickly hedgehog, by saying 'three friends'? I've only two, and the sooner I make an end of *them*, the better. Sally neglects me as it is, without having stupid mice to fuss over."

"My other friend isn't a mouse," said Pinny. "He's a mole."

"Oh yes, Sally did bring in a mole this morning," sniffed Snowflake. "She put him in Wilberforce's old cage, so you'll never see *him* again."

"Yes, I shall," grinned Pinny, "for you are going to help me set him free." Snowflake was much too surprised by this to say anything. "You see," went on Pinny, "if my friend the mole is shut up in that cage, Sally will be fussing over *him* instead of taking notice of *you*."

Snowflake knew this was true and she began to look at Pinny with respect. "Sally forgets all about me as it is," she sniffed, "and if she has another pet I know she'll forget me still more often. What do you want me to do? *I* can't open the cage with my big paws—I've often tried."

"That's where Wilberforce comes in," stated Pinny. "Mice have fingers; let both mice go and they'll open the cage and let the mole out."

"A good idea," purred Snowflake. "Then I can eat all three of them and Sally will only have me for a pet!"

Pinny's smile became wider than ever. "That's where you are mistaken, *dear* Mrs. Cat," he said. "You see, unless you promise to let them *all* go I will not let them rid you of that tiresome mole. Just think how fine it will be," he added, winking, "when there is nobody in the house for Sally to love but you."

Snowflake *did* think how fine it would be.

"Well—all right," she grumbled, "but you'll have to be fast, for I can hear Sally coming in from the garden."

And fast the friends were! A few moments later Diggy gave a start as someone said "Hello!" just outside the cage—and he saw it was Wilberforce smiling through the bars at him. "Give a push and the door should open," squeaked Wilberforce. It *did!* and soon the two mice were helping the mole to the floor. A white cat sat there, but she kept her head turned the other way;

and there, too, waiting by the door, was his old friend Pinny dancing with joy to see him safe. But the dancing stopped as they heard footsteps approaching along the hall.

"Why, there's my white mouse, and my mole—and two other animals running along the floor," cried Sally and she made a grab at one of them. Now this happened to be Pinny—and Sally forgot that hedgehogs have very sharp prickles!

"Ow!" cried Sally, and she tried to cram all her fingers into her mouth at the same time. Hand in hand Pinny and Ponsonby, and Wilberforce and Diggy hurried towards the door. Diggy was not really much of a runner but today he made his legs work like a steam-engine.

"I'll catch you, all of you, and have a zoo of my own!" shouted Sally, once again trying to catch them in her hands.

"Leave me, friends, for my legs don't move as fast as yours," panted the mole; but Wilberforce only grabbed his paw the tighter. Sally, almost tumbling over herself with excitement, drew nearer—and nearer.

Then, as they rushed down the garden path, Ponsonby saw that Hoppy and Mr. Heron stood in the shadow of the gate. He wondered whether Hoppy had managed to bring along Tippetty Nippet's sheet. Mr. Heron looked quite startled, as well he might, as the four creatures stumbled and shouted and squeaked their way towards him, a little girl close behind.

"Quickly, open the sheet!" squeaked Ponsonby, hoping wildly that Hoppy *had* brought it. But Hoppy had not forgotten. Quickly he unrolled the sheet and the four rolled onto it.

"H'm, a fine time to go to bed!" thought Pinny.

"Oh, Mr. Heron, please catch hold of the four corners—" gasped Ponsonby; and Hoppy at last knew what the hanky-sheet was for. Mr. Heron took the corners in his beak and rose swiftly into the air. Hoppy sailed up too, just as Sally reached the gate.

"Just in time!" he sang, watching the bulging sheet swinging from the Heron's beak like a sack of potatoes; then three heads popped out, smiling and calling "Goodbye!" to the little girl below. The fourth head, Pinny's, did not pop out. The others had piled their coats on top of him to save themselves from his prickles. As they were all standing on him he could not really enjoy the view.

That evening there was a party at Diggy's house. And what a party it was! Even Mr. Heron enjoyed himself, though he was so large he had to have his dandelion wine and honey cakes outside. As for Wilberforce, he laughed so much he almost split his new coat. How far away his life in the green cage seemed now. Ponsonby put everybody's thoughts into words when he raised his glass and said:

"May our friends Wilberforce and Diggy never, *never* be parted again! May they live

HAPPILY EVER AFTER!"

And did they?
Just look at the last picture and you will see.